# MARCO POLO &
# WELLINGTON
## *search for Solomon*

First published 1982
Copyright © 1982 by Janice Thompson
Jonathan Cape Ltd, 30 Bedford Square, London WC1

British Library Cataloguing in Publication Data

Thompson, Janice
Marco Polo and Wellington search for Solomon.
I. Title          II. Lewis, Naomi
823′.914[J]      · PZ7

ISBN 0-224-02036-6

Janice Thompson's original works of art
are exhibited exclusively by Portal Gallery Ltd,
London, England.

Printed in Italy by New Interlitho, SpA, Milan

# MARCO POLO & WELLINGTON
## *search for Solomon*

## JANICE THOMPSON & NAOMI LEWIS

JONATHAN CAPE THIRTY BEDFORD SQUARE LONDON

Once upon a time two good friends, a cat and a pig, lived happily on a farm. The pig was called Marco Polo, which was the name of a great traveller, long ago. Even when this pig was a tiny piglet he would wander off and explore. When the farmer found him the first time he said, "Well now, Marco Polo!" And the name stayed. The cat was called Wellington. Why? Because, even as a kitten he had so much disliked putting his paws in the mud that the farmer said, "You should be wearing wellies!" Puss didn't get Wellington boots, but he did keep the name.

There was a third friend too – a turkey called Solomon. One day, he and some other turkeys were driven away in a lorry. Marco and Wellington were most upset.

"We must go to his rescue," they said.

But how?

Cat and pig sat and thought. "We must look for him in a country called Turkey," said Wellington at last. "It lies far over the sea. To get to the sea we must hide in the back of the farmer's lorry. Tomorrow is his day for taking potatoes to seaside shops. We shall hide ourselves in sacks of potatoes and go too."

The plan worked – and there they were by the sea. The sun shone; the waves sparkled. Some children had left a bucket, spade and several flags; Marco Polo used all these to make some fine sand castles while Wellington went to ask a seagull if he knew the way to Turkey. When he returned he stood on his friend's back to keep his feet from the wet, and announced, "Marco, I can tell you our next move!"

"That seagull says," went on Wellington, "that we must cross to France, turn sideways and go straight on towards the morning sun. Now we must make a raft. Our sail will be this flag." He tied the flag to his tail.

When the raft was ready they carefully sat in the centre and Marco pushed it away from the shore with a long stick. They were afloat!

The night was rough, but some good-natured fish swam round and urged them on in the right direction. Then, at dawn, a wave washed them on to a quiet stretch of shore. "Sideways and then straight on," said Wellington. "We'll take that path over there."

The path led into a leafy forest. Suddenly Marco stopped. He looked pleased.

"Do you hear what I hear?" he asked.

Wellington paused. "I hear a snuffle, snuffle, snuffle," he said presently. But Marco had trotted ahead. And there, in a sunlit clearing, was a family of pigs. "Welcome, welcome!" they all cried, even the little ones. Then the largest held up his hoof. "We were expecting you. A seagull, an excellent fellow, flew by to tell us that you were coming. You must stay the night, of course; we are having truffles for supper. In the morning you head for Paris; all roads lead from there. After that, go on towards the morning sun until you see mountains. Then you can ask again."

Early next morning the pigs gave their guests a good breakfast and went with them to the far edge of the forest. "Follow the river!" they called, and waved until the travellers were out of sight. So Marco and Wellington padded away by the waterside until, after several days, they found themselves in a noisy city with traffic speeding by. "This must be Paris," said Wellington, "because there is the Eiffel Tower." He was a clever cat. But Marco did not care for heights and looked away. A man who was painting a picture by the river asked the pair to stop. He wanted to include them in the scene.

When he had finished he gave them some apples, cheese and bread, shook paw and hoof very warmly and wished the friends good luck.

They walked on until they were in the countryside, and went to sleep in a field.

They woke to bright sunshine. "We must make haste," said Wellington as he busily washed himself, and Marco tidied up their breakfast crumbs. They trotted on. The sun gave way to rain and mist. Sometimes, when the ground was wet, Marco Polo kindly offered his friend a lift on his back.

One day the view looked different. Before them was a range of snowcapped mountains – and these mountains had to be crossed. How ever would they manage it?

"If only pigs and cats could fly!" sighed Marco Polo.

"They can, you know!" A voice came from overhead. The friends looked up. There on a signpost was a beautiful ginger cat. With her was a bird.

The cat leapt neatly down.

"We have been waiting for you," said the cat, whose name was Josephine. "We heard of you from a seagull. My friend here," (she waved a paw towards the bird), "knows where a balloon is waiting to take you over the Alps. It leaves in an hour's time. Come now." She set off briskly. The others followed, while the bird flew on ahead. And there was the great balloon, swaying about, with its basket on the ground.

"In you get," said the cat. "You will find a picnic lunch inside. When I untie the ropes you'll rise at once. You should land near Venice. When you arrive, ask for my uncle Garibaldi. Don't forget."

"Thank you, thank you," the travellers cried. "If ever you need a friend –"

But their words were lost as they soared into the sky.

Up, up, up went the balloon. Wellington was excited, but Marco covered his face with his hoofs. *He* preferred exploring on the ground.

"Look! There's Mont Blanc!" said Wellington. "It's the highest peak in the Alps!" But Marco just peeped out, then covered his eyes again. When at last he opened them the mountains had been crossed, and they were landing on a grassy slope.

As they climbed out a wild goose flew to meet them. "You've been quick," she said. "That's good. A bird from over the mountains told me to wait for you and point out the road to Venice. That's the way, over there. Don't forget to ask for Garibaldi. Now I must go."

Before they had time to thank her, off she had flown.

The two friends padded on, singing, in turn, all the songs they could remember. Marco sang about pigs, and Wellington sang about cats.

And then they found themselves in a place where the streets were all made of water, and the buildings looked like very old, crumbling palaces. "Ah, yes – Venice," said Wellington. "And those boats are called gondolas. You get in that one, I'll get in this. And look out for Garibaldi."

At last they reached a small paved square which seemed to be full of cats. "Here's a likely place," said Wellington. They drew in to the bank and clambered out. Marco looked for pigs, but there were none. Meanwhile, Wellington asked the nearest cat if he knew Garibaldi.

"Of course! There he is by the pump."

Garibaldi, a wise old cat, rose to greet him. "Ah," said he, "you must tell me about my niece, Josephine, over the mountains. But first I will give you a message. Listen carefully."

"You are near the end of your search," said Garibaldi. "Your next stop will be Turkey. To get there you will travel on a train called the Orient Express; it leaves Venice this evening. I'll take you to the station and see you safely started. On the way you will tell me your story."

They reached the station and boarded the train in good time. It was a ride to remember! Wellington kept in his mind the splendid names of the stations that they passed: Trieste, Belgrade, Sofia – what a journey! At sunrise they saw mountains and – flying past, could that be their friend, the wild goose?

Then the train came to a halt at Istanbul. They were in Turkey.

"What do we do now?" asked Marco. As he spoke, a snow-white cat stepped out of the shadows and beckoned them with his paw.

"My name is Florizel," said the cat. "A wild goose – an excellent bird – told me to look for you. Here is the news of your friend Solomon. He escaped from the lorry and flew into a walled garden. This garden belongs to an odious carpet dealer who is greatly disliked for his vanity, greed and bad temper. This man wears a bright red fez in which he sticks a fresh turkey feather each day. He takes the feathers from Solomon, and keeps him locked in a tiny cage. Follow me."

The white cat led them through narrow, twisting streets and stopped at a high-walled garden with iron gates. The animals peered through. There was Solomon, in a cage, just as they had been told.

The two cats looked round cautiously, then climbed into the garden, while Marco stayed on guard. Then Wellington used a claw to pick the lock of the cage – he was a clever cat!

Solomon shook the cramp from his wings and thanked his rescuers, "Listen," he whispered. "There is a room inside where some special magic carpets are kept, and they will take us home. Come very quietly."

They had all just reached the secret room when they heard the dealer's steps. The whole place shook with his rage. "I'll lock you up for ever more!" he shouted, and pounced at the animals. The feathers flew! But, with Solomon's aid, they pushed a sack over his head and tied him up as well as they could. By the time he had freed himself they were sure to be safely in the air.

Would they be, though? There the friends sat, cat, pig and turkey, each on a magic carpet, but they did not move. They had to utter certain magic words to make the carpets start – and Solomon *could not remember what those words were*.

"Let us be calm," said Wellington. "Let us sit on our carpets and think hard. Then we will try out magical words in turn." So they began:

"Open Sesame!"

"Abra cadabra!"

"Grand Vizier!"

"Marzipan!"

"Turkish Delight!"

"Sherbet-Dip!"

"Rise, oh magic carpets!"

At the last (uttered by Wellington, a clever cat as we know) the carpets stirred and rose, and the animals just had time to call goodbye to Florizel before they were skimming over bazaars and cities, rivers and mountains, forest and ocean – the whole of their amazing journey spread beneath them like a map. They hoped that their many good friends below would see them as they waved.